Miss D. ...y-Jane was ever so vain

by Julie Fulton

Illustrated by Jona Jung

Miss Dorothy-Jane was **ever so vain.**
She **stared** in her **mirror** for hours.
Was her hair brushed just right? Was her jumper too tight?
Would her hat look much **better** with flowers?

When she went into town she would strut up and down,
thinking **people** would see her and smile.
That they'd say with **delight**, 'What a wonderful sight
to see **somebody** dress with such style.'

NEW TOWN HALL

DE LADY
QUEEN
TO WEL...
FOR GRAND OPENING
of TOWN HALL
on JUNE 30th

HAMILTON SHADY
WILL NEED ITS BEST LADY
TO CURTSEY AND WELCOME

It was sunny and so she **decided** to go
for a **stroll** to the town's brand new hall.
She could see a large crowd, people shouting out loud
at a **poster** nailed up on the wall.

It said, 'Hamilton Shady will need its best lady to curtsey and welcome the Queen.
If you think you're the best, come along with the rest and join the parade on the green.'

A dress or a **skirt?** Her red blouse or a shirt?
Off she rushed to pick out a new **bow.**
Her **pink** or blue shoes? There was so much to choose,
but at last she was ready to go.

Feeling sure she would win, she jumped out of her skin when a **seagull** swooped over her head.
It pooed as it passed, but she stepped aside fast so it splattered the **pavement** instead.

As she **walked** by the zoo a sea lion named Lou
flipped his fish really **high** in the air.
'Put your parasol up,' shouted **keeper McCrupp**,
'or it's going to land in your hair!'

She straightened her hat, crept around a **black cat**,
stepped with care past a fresh-painted seat.
Then a **sports car** roared by, sending water sky high,
which came splashing down right by her feet.

Miss Dorothy-Jane, who was ever so vain,
checked **herself** from her head to her toes.
'I mustn't be late or arrive in a state!'
But, on turning the corner, she **froze**.

In the pond, on a **log**, was a little black dog.
It was **trembling** and shaking with fear.
It fell in with a yelp so she shouted out, **'Help!'**
But **none** of the people could hear.

'Oh my goodness,' she cried, as she watched from the sid
'there **really** is no time to lose.

The dog's starting to **sink**.' Without stopping to think,
Miss Dorothy kicked off her shoes.

'The poor dog will **drown!**' she cried out with a frown
and forgot the parade on the green.
She dived in, pulled it out, and then started to **shout,**
'I don't **think** I will **ever** get clean!'

She sat down in **tears**, but soon heard lots of cheers.
'We choose you to welcome the Queen.
You've got weeds on your toes, mud and **slime** on your nose,
but you're the **best** person we've ever seen!'

Miss Dorothy-Jane was no **longer** so vain.

She made **lots** of new friends in the town.

They all shouted 'Hooray!' when she gave the bouquet

and the **Queen smiled** from under her **crown.**

The End

Miss Dorothy-Jane Was Ever So Vain
An original concept by Julie Fulton
© Julie Fulton

Illustrator: Jona Jung
Jona Jung is represented
by MSM Studio www.msmstudio.eu

Published by MAVERICK ARTS PUBLISHING LTD

3A Horsham City Business Centre,
Brighton Road, Horsham, West Sussex, RH13 5BB
© Maverick Arts Publishing Limited September 2013 + 44 (0) 1403 256941

A CIP catalogue record for this book is available from the British Library.

ISBN 978-1 -84886-106-0

Maverick
arts publishing

www.maverickbooks.co.uk